For Ned. xxx

Text and illustrations copyright © Sarah Dyer 2017
The right of Sarah Dyer to be identified as the author and illustrator
of this work has been asserted by her in accordance with the
Copyright, Designs and Patents Act, 1988 (United Kingdom).

First published in Great Britain and in the USA in 2017 by
Otter-Barry Books, Little Orchard, Burley Gate, Herefordshire, HR1 3QS
www.otterbarrybooks.com

A catalogue record for this book is available from the British Library.

ISBN 978-1-91095-908-4

Illustrated with mixed media and collage

Printed in China

9 8 7 6 5 4 3 2 1

Monster Baby

Sarah Dyer

Otter-Barry BOOKS

Mum says she's going to have a baby.

Dad says it's a good thing,
but Scamp and I aren't so sure.

Mum needs to rest and eat **lots** of healthy food.

This means
we have to as well.

But Mum doesn't seem
to be getting
any thinner.

Maybe she's resting too much.

I am a bit sad that Mum can't carry me any more.

The hospital put jelly on
Mum's **huge BIG** tummy,
and we saw the baby
on a screen.

I thought it looked more like a wiggly worm.

I wish the baby would come out soon, but Mum says it won't be ready for a few more months.

Mum says the baby can already
hear us, so I try and talk to it.

At last the baby is coming!
Granny comes to stay with us
so Dad can take Mum to
the hospital.

Hooray!
The baby is here at last!
I go to visit Mum
in the hospital.

Dad says that now
the baby monster
is here I am a
BIG monster.

I ask Scamp if
I've grown.

I **think** I'm glad to have Mum back home, and the new baby. But I have to play quietly, even though the baby is allowed to make as much noise as he likes.

Meh meh mehh meee Wah Waah Waaaah

Lots of people come to visit
and the baby gets **LOTS** of presents.

I get some presents too, but I feel
a bit left out – and so does Scamp.

But the baby is
interested in me.
Very interested!

I think he **likes** me.

And I **think** I like him, too.

In fact, I can't wait to share
EVERYTHING
with my monster baby brother!